World of Reading

LEVEL 2

THE STORY OF
SPIDER-MAN

Adapted by Thomas Macri
Illustrated by The Storybook Art Group
Based on the Marvel comic book series Spider-Man

MARVEL
New York • Los Angeles

marvelkids.com

© 2012 MARVEL

Printed in the United States of America

First Edition

9 10 8

FAC-029261-19330

ISBN 978-1-4231-5409-9

Peter Parker didn't have
many friends.

Other kids thought Peter was different. They made fun of him. They liked sports and music. Peter liked books.

Peter loved all his classes at school.
But he loved science the most.

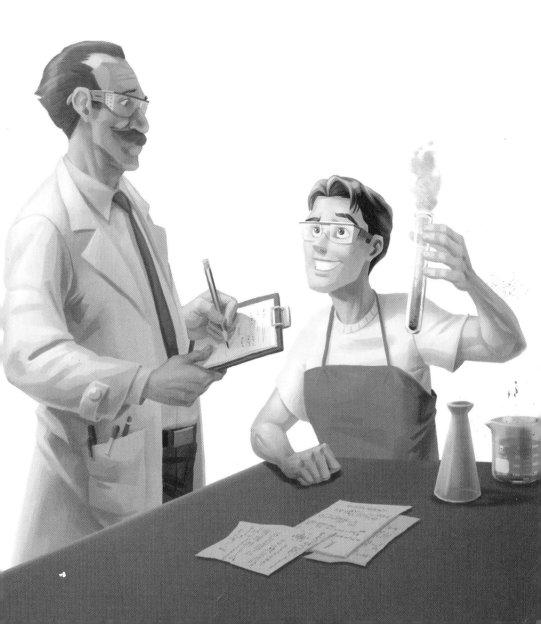

Peter only loved one thing more than science. He loved his family. He lived with his Aunt May and his Uncle Ben. At home, Peter couldn't have been happier.

Aunt May and Uncle Ben loved Peter. They bought him a new microscope. Uncle Ben told him that science was power. "And," he said, "with great power comes great responsibility."

One day, Peter heard that a lab was going to do something special. They were going to show how rays worked. Peter visited the lab to see it.

The rays lit up. But a spider dropped down between them.

The spider was zapped with power.

Peter didn't notice something.
The spider was falling down. And
it was falling on him!

The spider was glowing with power.
It bit Peter's hand.

Peter held his head. He felt sick.

Peter left the lab. He felt so sick
that he almost didn't see a car
coming.

He jumped out of the way.

He jumped higher than he thought
he could. He landed on a wall.
And he stuck to it!

He climbed up the wall. He was just like the spider that bit him!

He jumped from roof to roof. His
powers were like a spider's.
He must have gotten them from the
spider's bite!

Peter was amazed by his powers.

Peter saw a poster of a wrestler.
He would test his powers on him.

Peter put on a mask. He challenged the wrestler.

He threw the wrestler.

He beat the wrestler!

Peter was happy. But he couldn't
be a spider-man without something
else. He went home and made some
gluey stuff.

Then he made something to shoot
the stuff. He called them
web-shooters.

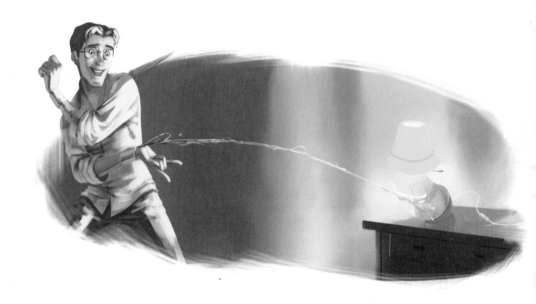

Peter made a costume. He called himself Spider-Man!

People loved Spider-Man! They loved
his powers. Soon he was famous.

But one night he saw a robbery taking place. A cop called out to stop the crook. But Peter didn't stop him. Peter was tired of being told what to do. So he let the crook go.

Peter went home. There were cops
outside. He knew something
was wrong. The cops told Peter
there had been a crime at his house.
Uncle Ben was the victim.

Peter put on his Spider-Man costume.

He rushed to find the criminal.

When he found him, Peter discovered
something terrible. The crook was
the same man he had let run away.

Peter was so sad he cried. But he remembered that Uncle Ben had told him with great power comes great responsibility.

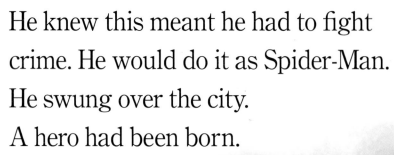

He knew this meant he had to fight
crime. He would do it as Spider-Man.
He swung over the city.
A hero had been born.